The SHOEMAKER and the ELVES

Retold and illustrated by

Cynthia and William Birrer

Lothrop, Lee & Shepard Books   New York

For Eve

Library of Congress Cataloging in Publication Data. Birrer, Cynthia. The shoemaker
and the elves. Adaptation of: Wichtelmänner. Summary: A poor old shoemaker
becomes successful with the help of two elves who finish his shoes during the
night. [1. Fairy tales. 2. Folklore—Germany] I. Birrer, William, ill.
II. Wichtelmänner. III. Title. PZ8.B55Sh 1983 398.2'1'0943
[E] 83-1145 ISBN 0-688-01988-9 ISBN 0-688-01989-7 (lib. bdg.)

Once upon a time
there was a poor
but kindly shoemaker
and his wife.

They lived in a village, above their little shop.

One day the shoemaker found he had
enough leather for only one pair of shoes.
He cut out the pieces that evening.

He and his wife then said their prayers
and went to bed. He would make the
shoes in the morning.

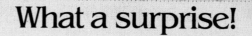
What a surprise!

The next morning he found a finely crafted, finished pair of shoes on the table.

Soon a customer came in. He was so pleased with the beautiful shoes that he paid more than the usual price for them.

With the money, the shoemaker bought enough leather for two pairs of shoes.

He cut out the pieces that evening so he could make the shoes the next morning.

When the shoemaker and his wife awoke,
they found that two beautiful pairs of
shoes had been made.

These were soon sold, and with the money the shoemaker bought enough leather for four pairs of shoes.

He cut out the pieces for the four pairs of
shoes in the evening, and once again
found them complete in the morning.

And so it went on. Everyone came to buy the good

old man's shoes, and soon he became quite rich.

Then, one evening near Christmas, after he had finished his cutting out, the shoemaker said to his wife,

"Let us stay up tonight, dear, and see who has been helping us."

So they decided to hide in the next room
and peep through a crack in the door.

Exactly at midnight, two small, naked
men slipped quickly through the door,

climbed onto the table, and started to
work on the shoes.

They stitched,
they sewed,
they hammered
so skillfully and

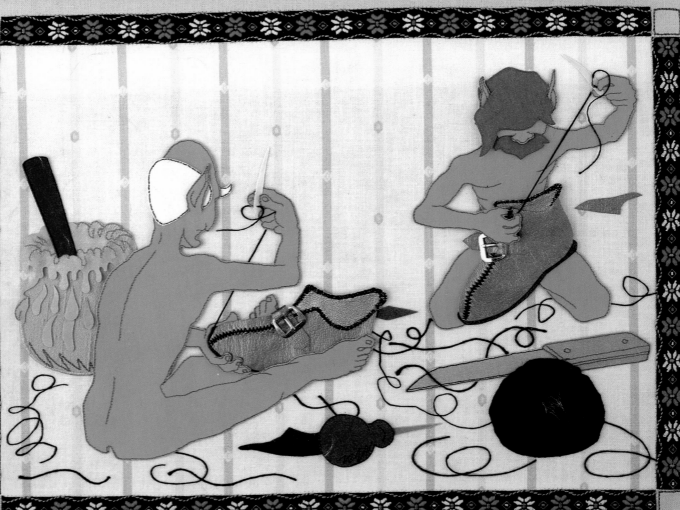

quickly that the
shoemaker and
his wife could
not help staring.

When all was done, the little men
leaped off the table and disappeared
into the night.

The next morning the wife said to the shoemaker,

"The little men have made us rich, but they have no clothes. Let us make them something to wear."

So she made two fine suits of clothes
with knitted stockings and caps, and the

shoemaker made two tiny pairs of shoes
and two leather belts.

When everything was ready, they

laid it all out neatly on the table.

Then they hid and waited to see what would happen.

Promptly at midnight, the two naked men came bounding in.

Up onto the table they climbed.

How astonished they were to find splendid clothes instead of pieces of leather!

Overjoyed, they hopped about and
dressed themselves quickly.

Skipping and dancing, they sang,
"The kindly old folks have set us free,
So no longer now must we cobblers be!"

Then they skipped out into the night and were seen no more.

And the good shoemaker and his wife
lived in happiness and prosperity for the
rest of their lives.

DATE			